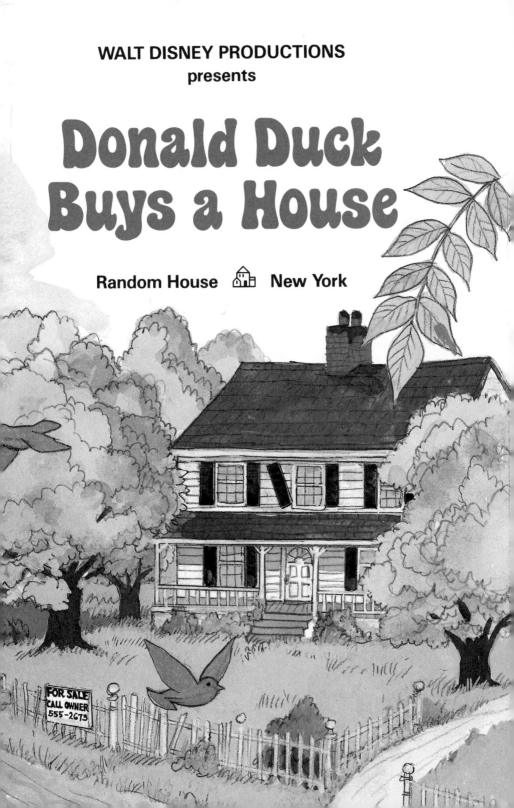

WALT DISNEY PRODUCTIONS
presents

Donald Duck Buys a House

Random House New York

It was a beautiful summer day.
Donald was driving in the country.
He passed by an old empty house.
All of a sudden Donald stopped.
A sign was nailed to the fence.
Did the sign say FOR SALE?
Yes, it did!

Donald backed up the car and got out.

He peered
in a window.
The house
was very old.
It needed
lots of work.

But Donald could just see it now. . . .
He was lying in a hammock.
Daisy was bringing lemonade.
The boys were playing in the yard.
What a life that would be!

In a flash Donald was back
in his car, heading for town.

Donald told Huey,
Dewey, and Louie
all about the house.
Then he called
the owner.

Before Donald knew it, he had bought
the house.
"Well, boys, soon we will spend
our holidays there,"
Donald said.

"May we go to see the house now, Uncle Donald?" asked the boys.

"No," Donald said. "First I have to fix it up. Nobody has lived there for a long time."

But Donald was wrong.
Somebody was living there.
Two chipmunks, Chip and Dale,
had made a nest in a room
downstairs.

The chipmunks were gathering food
for the winter.

They had put nuts in an old tree.

Now they were busy bringing the nuts
into the house.

The next day, Donald got ready
to work on his new house.

He loaded up his car
and off he drove.

When Donald got to the house, Chip
and Dale were running out a window.
Donald did not see the chipmunks,
and they did not see him.

Donald lugged his ladder and paint
into the front hall.

He opened up
the paint can.
Now he was
ready to begin.

Then Donald saw the chipmunks' mess.
"Oh, boy!" he said. "I see I have
a lot of work to do. I'll get started
right away."

Donald found
a wastebasket,
a dustpan, and
a broom.

He swept up the leaves and
nuts and threw them away.
He did not know he had swept
away the chipmunks' home.

Donald cleared away
the cobwebs.
Finally he was ready
to paint.

He painted
all the windows.
When he was done,
Donald went to bed.

My, was
he tired!

Soon after, Chip and Dale came home.
"Where did our nest go?" cried Chip.
"It was here when we left!"

The chipmunks jumped
to the floor.

They knocked over
the can of yellow paint.
"Where did this paint
come from?" asked Dale.

All at once they heard a noise
coming from upstairs.
"Someone is here!" said Dale.
"Let's go look!"

As they ran upstairs
they knocked over a can
of blue paint.
They left a trail
of tiny footprints.
The strange noise
was growing
louder.

Very slowly Chip and Dale opened the door.

There was Donald, snoring.

"Come on!" said Dale. "We must get out of here before he wakes up!"

And off they raced.

Chip and Dale ran to the nearest nut tree.
It had a hole with leaves and nuts inside.
"I miss our old home," Dale said sadly.
"This will have to do for now," said Chip.

All night the chipmunks sat eating nuts
and throwing shells onto the roof below.
"I hope that duck goes away soon so we
can have our old home back," said Dale.

PING! PING! PING!
Donald woke up.
What was that noise?

Donald sat up.
Was it a ghost?
Or maybe there were
robbers in the house!

Donald hid under the covers.
The sound went on and on.
He did not get a wink
of sleep all night.

The next morning
Donald came downstairs
tired and grumpy.

What a mess he saw!
There was paint and small footprints
everywhere.

Donald followed
the footprints until
he came to a tree.
There sat Chip
and Dale!

"Aha! You made
this mess and
the noise, too!"
shouted Donald.
"I'll get you
yet!"

"I think I have a plan," Donald said to himself.

First he sawed a hole in a broken floorboard.

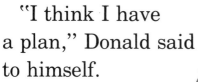

He put an empty bag with a long string into the hole.

Then Donald
covered the hole
with a scarf.

Next Donald took a bag of nuts.
He left a trail
of nuts from the trap
to the window sill.

It was not long
before Chip and
Dale spotted
the nuts.

They followed
the trail of nuts
to the scarf.

Then, all at once, down they fell
into the bag!

"That mean duck!"
cried Chip. "He set
this trap."

"Well, I know a way
to get out!" said Dale.
He showed Chip how
to chew through the bag.

Soon the chipmunks
were free.
Off they raced.

Donald soon found
the empty bag.
He was really mad!

"I will get those
chipmunks if it's
the last thing I do!"
Donald cried.

Donald got a box.

He got a bell, some string, and a stick.
He built a bigger and better trap.

Donald sat down to wait
for the chipmunks.
But Donald was very tired.
Soon he fell fast asleep.

A little while later,
the chipmunks spotted
the nuts under the box.

"I bet it's a trap,"
said Dale.

"If we are careful,
we can get the nuts,"
said Chip.

The chipmunks ran
down the tree.

But a porcupine
came along just then.

He scared Chip
and Dale away.

The porcupine saw the nuts too.
He grabbed for them.
The stick fell over and down came the box.

RING! RING!
went the bell.

"Wow!" said Dale. "It really *is* a trap!"

The bell woke up
Donald.
    He jumped out
of his seat.

He ran to the box.
"Oh, boy! Now I've got you!"
he shouted happily.

Donald lifted the box just a little.
"Come out, you miserable chipmunks!"
he said.

The porcupine leaped out
of the box and knocked
Donald down.

Ouch! Donald was covered
with quills.

"I have had it!"
Donald shouted.
"I'm leaving!"

Soon Donald was packed and
ready to go.

Just then a car drove up.

Out stepped Daisy and
Huey, Dewey, and Louie.

They were carrying
sleeping bags and
lots of food.

"Donald, where are you going?"
asked Daisy. "We've come to visit."

"You can stay, but I am leaving,"
said Donald.

He pointed to the tree.

"Those chipmunks have been living
in the house. They make
a terrible mess. And they
keep me up all night."

"Look, the chipmunks were here before you," Daisy said to Donald. "This was their home. You chased them out. Why don't you build them another home instead?"

"That's an idea," said Donald.
"We'll help!" said Huey, Dewey, and Louie.
The boys and Donald got tools and wood.

They went to work right away.
Soon the house looked like a house.
Then they painted it blue.

"Let's put it in the tree," said Dewey.

Now everyone was happy.

The chipmunks had a new home and so did Donald.

His dream had come true.

"There was always enough room around here for the chipmunks," Daisy told Donald. "You just had to find enough room for them in your heart."